The Gingerbread Man

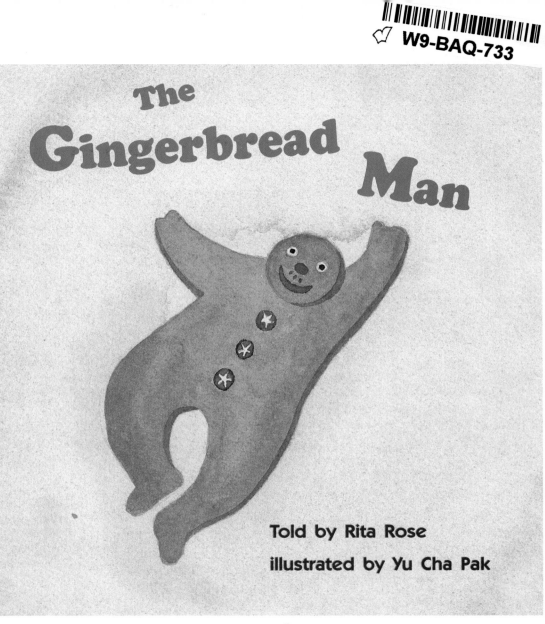

Told by Rita Rose

illustrated by Yu Cha Pak

GReaT SOuRCe
EDUCATION GROUP
A Houghton Mifflin Company

Once upon a time, an old woman and an old man baked a gingerbread man.

The gingerbread man ran away!

The old woman and the old man
ran after the gingerbread man.

"Run, run, as fast as you can.
You can't catch me.
I'm the gingerbread man,"
he called.

A cow and a horse ran after
the gingerbread man.

"Run, run, as fast as you can.
You can't catch me.
I'm the gingerbread man,"
he called.

A farmer and her husband ran after
the gingerbread man.

"Run, run, as fast as you can.
You can't catch me.
I'm the gingerbread man,"
he called.

Then the gingerbread man came to a river.
Where could he run now?

Just then a fox jumped out of the bushes.
"Jump on my back," said the fox.
The gingerbread man jumped
on the fox's back.

"Jump on my head," said the fox.
The gingerbread man jumped
on the fox's head.

"Jump on my nose," said the fox.
The gingerbread man jumped
on the fox's nose.

SNIP, SNAP.

That was the end of the gingerbread man.